M000298125

CAN MAN

KILLER OF COP-KILLERS

BOOK THREE

A NOVELLA BY JOHN DITTO

ISBN: 978-1-7343501-0-4
email: canman@reagan.com

Acknowledgments

Special thanks to **TREVOR OWEN**.

Introduction

In book three, Jack is after a cop killer or cop killers. Whichever it is, it will be dangerous for the Can Man.

Chapter One

Jack leaned against the bar and thought, *Wow! What a roller coaster ride my life's been with all the ups and downs. Sometimes life has come at me steep and sometimes fast and sometimes a little of both.* He looked up at the clock on the wall near the front door of his pub.

It was after 4 o'clock and all of his early regulars were gone and the off-duty police officers should start coming in soon. This was always the quiet time in the pub.

There was a crashing at the front door. A Hispanic girl rushed in screaming and crying for help. Her blouse was torn and there were bloody marks on her face and arms. Jack ran from behind the bar to catch her as she fell.

"What happened to you? Catch your breath. You are safe now," said Jack.

Jack sat her down at one of the nearby tables. After a few moments of her trying to calm down, she looked up at Jack and said, "You have to help that policeman."

Jack asked, "What policeman?"

After gulping in some more air, the frightened girl pointed down towards the bayou that ran about a block behind Jack's pub.

About that time, Chief Mike and Officer Taylor walked in. When they saw the condition of the girl, they immediately sprang into action. Chief Mike called for back-up and an EMT to the pub. The young Hispanic girl told the Chief her name was Lupe and that she was riding her bicycle down the sidewalk that runs along the side of bayou when a group of Hispanic gangbangers rushed out from underneath the overpass and grabbed her and her bicycle. They laughed and shouted in Spanish, "We are going to rape you."

She fought them as best she could but there were too many of them.

Chief Mike asked, "How many?"

"My guess, maybe six," the girl replied.

The Chief radioed in for his units to converge on the location she described.

Lupe grabbed Chief Mike's arm and told him, "Hurry. A policeman came to my rescue when he heard my screams from under the overpass. It's because of him I was able to get away."

Mike's eyes widened. "Are you telling me that a police officer is down there with a street gang of six by himself?"

Lupe put her head down and said, "Yes."

The Chief picked up his radio again and shouted, "Officer in distress!" Then he gave the location. He turned his attention back to Lupe. He told her that he and Officer Taylor had to leave but for her to stay put in the pub. The EMTs were on their way.

The Chief looked up at Jack and said, "Stay with her."

Jack responded, "I'll watch over her until help arrives."

The two police officers rushed out of the pub and headed down to the bayou to find the officer. Within moments, the paramedics arrived and started tending to Lupe's wounds.

Jolene, one of the pub's waitresses arrived. "What's happening here, Jack?"

"There was an attempted rape and maybe an injured police officer. Listen, Jolene. This all happened near here. Right behind the pub down by the bayou. Would you mind watching the place while I walk down there and see what's going on?"

"Of course, I'll watch the pub. You go," Jolene said.

Jack hit the door and walked at a pretty good stride. He arrived at the location the girl described and saw lots of police cars and yellow tape already blocking off a large area under the overpass. Jack knew most of the cops there but still respected their tape. He stopped and waited until one of them walked over.

Jack asked, "What happened?"

The young cop said, "There was a murder."

Jack's heart sank. This is the worst news possible. He was afraid to even ask who? The young cop walked on by. Jack was sick. He knew that the odds were it was an officer he had probably served a beer to at his pub. Looking back towards the crime scene he spotted Chief Mike who waved him over. Jack ducked under the yellow tape and walked over to him.

Chief Mike asked, "Is Lupe okay?"

"The paramedics are seeing to her wounds," said Jack. "I hate to ask but who was the police officer who got murdered?"

The Chief put his hand on Jack's shoulder and said, "It wasn't a police officer."

Jack was puzzled. "But Lupe said a policeman came to her rescue."

"She was mistaken," said Chief Mike. "It wasn't a policeman. It was a parking meter reader. They have similar uniforms with a badge but no firearm."

Jack thought, *poor guy. He charged in to help that young girl and ended up getting killed himself.*

The detectives were already on the scene. They took photographs and talked to witnesses. Jack knew they would be headed to his place to talk to Lupe. At least there wouldn't be any yellow tape around his pub. Jack shook the Chief's hand and said he needed to get back to work.

Chapter Two

Back at the pub, Jack saw Lupe had numerous bandages and two gauze patches on her arm.

A detective walked in and asked Jack, "Is that her?"

"Yes," said Jack. "That's her."

"We need to get her statement," said the detective.

"Sure," said Jack.

After getting debriefed by the detective, Lupe was released, and a police unit took her home. Suzanna's Pub was back to normal. Except there weren't any off-duty police officers there. That didn't surprise Jack, with the murder happening so close to his pub. He told Jolene and Betsy they could take the night off and they both took him up on the offer.

Jack wiped down the bar like he always did and began to ask himself questions. Should the Can Man get involved with this murder?

It was a meter reader who risked his life and died trying to rescue a girl he didn't even know. Jack saw similarities between the meter reader shooting and the shooting of Officer Stevens, the officer who was shot shielding Jack's wife from bullets that ended up killing them both. He decided long ago to keep a narrow focus on eliminating cop killers, and that's it. The police were capable of keeping law and order without his help. But he felt like this was different.

Could it be that the street gang thought the meter reader was a cop because of his uniform? Parking enforcement is a branch of the Police Department. The longer he thought about it the more he thought he should do something about that street gang.

Jack knew the gang killed the meter reader with knives, but he didn't know if there was one killer or many. He decided to do what he always does, listen to the cops in his pub. After four days, Jack realized they didn't know any more than he did.

Monday morning rolled around. Jose drove up in his beer delivery truck. Jack wondered if maybe, by a long shot, Jose heard something in the Hispanic community.

Jose walked back through the pub with his empty dolly and stopped to chat. It was a hot day. Jack offered him a cold bottle of water on the house.

After taking a long swig, Jose said, "Thanks for the water. It's just what I needed."

Jack said, "You are welcome."

Then Jack cleared his throat and asked the long-shot question. "Did you hear about the murder behind the pub down by the bayou? Apparently, it was a Hispanic street gang."

Oh, yes," said Jose. "At my church we all are aware of the gang members and afraid of them. They are very bad men up from South America."

Jack was happy to get this info. He said, "Please go on, Jose."

Jose said, "It is very dangerous for me to even be talking to you about them. They would kill me and my family if they knew."

Jack could see the real fear in Jose's eyes and decided to let him say what he wanted to say. No pushing for extra info.

Jack said, "Don't worry, Jose. This conversation will not go beyond these four walls."

Jose moved closer to Jack and said, "The leader is a very, very, bad man. His name is Lobo. But when he is not around, everyone just calls him Mad Dog." Jose stopped to nervously take a sip of water. Looking around he continued to tell Jack what he had heard.

"Lobo came to the US with two of his friends. Supposedly, the three grew up together on the streets of a large slum in South America. They had no parents and the gang became their family. Lobo developed a bad habit of robbing and stealing. That's how he survived."

Jack said, "I see. Go on."

"One day, Lobo tried to rob a man who worked on floors. When Lobo came at him, the man pulled out his linoleum knife. That really got Lobo's attention. Then the rest of his gang showed up and they overpowered the man. Lobo took the linoleum knife for himself. He liked the idea that it was scary. After using it a few times, he discovered that he didn't like the round wood handle. It was awkward. He wanted a handle that was more like a knife handle."

Jose took another sip of water and continued. "Lobo knew of a kid who went to a high school that had a metal shop. The kid told Lobo that he could fasten the linoleum knife blade onto a knife handle. All he asked for in return was that he and his family to be left alone. They both shook on it."

Jack said, "So, he has a special knife! Go on."

"Lobo developed another bad habit. He took great pleasure in slicing open his victims' stomachs with his new knife. As time went on, the gang got bolder and bolder, robbing people in the middle of the day in plain sight of everyone. After many complaints, the police decided to rid their city of this gang. They decided to place police officers at both ends of the street where many people had been robbed. Two police officers dressed up as a tourist couple, complete with shopping bags. As they walked down the sidewalk in front of the local businesses, sure enough, the gang members converged on them from all sides."

Jack said, "So the police laid a trap for them."

Jose said, "Yes, Mr. Jack. And when they were almost upon them, the two officers dropped their shopping bags, with pistols already in their hands. The gang froze for a second, then scattered. That's when the other police who were in hiding, sprang into action with their guns drawn. It was chaos. Lots of gunshots were fired. Lobo and his two friends were the only ones able to escape. The South American police force had some soldiers mixed in with them. They shot and killed all of the other gang members. To them, they were the enemy of the country. One of those killed was one of Lobo's best friends. Lobo knew they had to leave. Coming to America seemed to be a good idea. Lobo's hatred of the police grew and grew. Then last week when his new gang tried to rape that lady and that man came to help her, Lobo saw the uniform and thought he was a cop."

Jack said, "So that's why they killed him?

Jose nodded yes.

Jack started to ask Jose more questions, but Jose said he really had to go. More bars were waiting for their beer deliveries. The little bell above the door rang as Jose left.

Chapter Three

Jack was happy with all the new info he received. There was a lot he had to think about. One thing was for sure now, Lobo was a cop killer and Can Man was the one to take care of that Mad Dog!

The next few days were pretty ordinary. The same daytime regulars arrived followed by the off-duty police officers. Two police officers down at the end talked about the gang murder.

As Jack eased closer to hear the conversation, one of cops looked up and said, "Hey Jack. Could you come here for minute?"

Wow, Jack thought. *He went from trying to ease drop to being invited.*

The two were Officers Martinez and Alford. They both shook Jack's hand. Officer Martinez said, "Hey Jack. Remember that Hispanic girl that got attacked and then ran in here for help?"

Jack responded, "Of course. I hope she's doing all right."

Officer Alford said, "She's recovering well. Her mom came to the station today to thank us for all the help we gave Lupe. She said she would come here to personally thank you your help. As a matter of fact, I think that's them coming in right now."

Jack immediately recognized Lupe. She ran over and gave him a big hug, then introduced her mom, Anna.

Jack sat them down at a table. Jolene asked the two ladies what they would like to drink. They both responded that light beer would be fine.

Jack said, "Jolene, their drinks are on the house." Jolene nodded.

Lupe said, "I told my mom how you helped me after I was attacked. She said she wanted to thank you personally."

Jack turned to Anna and said, "I was glad to help."

"Where's the ladies room?" Anna asked.

Lupe and Jack both pointed her in the right direction. Jack knew this might be a rare opportunity to get some more info on this Lobo guy. He decided to forget the tact and come out and ask direct questions. Time was short before her mom returned.

Jack asked, "Lupe, would you mind telling me what you know about this Lobo guy?"

Her expression went from a smile to a frightened serious look. Lupe leaned in and said in a whisper, "He is a very dangerous man. And I'm afraid to speak of him to anyone."

Jack thought that this was the same fear he saw in his beer delivery man, Jose. But he urged her on.

"My pub is one block away from where your attack happened and where that meter reader was murdered. I would like to know what he looks like. He can walk in here and I wouldn't even know it's him. So please, at least, tell me what he looks like. And maybe describe his tattoos or other identifying marks."

Lupe whispered, "Lobo has no tattoos. He has sandy colored curly hair and is a little on the heavy side."

Jack leaned back with a surprised look on his face. "Are you sure we are talking about the same guy?"

Lupe said, "Yes I know. He looks completely different than all of his gang members."

Wow, Jack thought. *He actually could have been in his pub, and he wouldn't have even known it.*

Jack knew Lupe's mom would be back any minute, so he wanted to confirm one more thing.

"I heard he uses a modified linoleum knife to kill his victims. He gets some kind of thrill cutting their throats with it. Is that true?"

Lupe's mom was on her way back to their table. Lupe quickly looked back at Jack and whispered, "No he cuts their bellies open."

Lupe leaned back in her chair and smiled at her mom as she sat back down. She asked, "Are you ready to go?"

Her mom looked surprised. "We haven't even finished our first beer."

Lupe stood up and told her, "Mom I don't feel well and I really want to go home. You got to meet Jack and I've been through a lot lately."

Jack stood up and shook both of their hands and said, "Thank you for coming in. It was nice to meet you and see you again, Lupe. I'm glad you are okay and thank you for our little talk."

As the two ladies walked away, Jack overheard Lupe's mom ask, "What little talk?"

Chapter Four

Jack went back behind the bar. Between Lupe and Jose, Jack had learned a lot about this Lobo guy. And Lobo was at the top of the Can Man's list. The phone rang and it was Heather. When Jack heard her voice, it occurred to him that he hadn't paid much attention to her lately and was probably in trouble.

Heather asked, "Are we still dating? I haven't heard from you in a while."

Jack apologized. "I'm sorry. I'm sorry. There was a murder a block behind the pub and it's been a little crazy around here."

Heather said, "Well Jack, that's a police matter, isn't it? I thought we had something special."

Jack knew Heather was trying to get him to assure her that she was the most important thing in his life. Then the words spilled out. "Heather, I really, really, care about you. But I have a business to run and there was a murder one block behind it. If you don't understand my concern, then maybe we ought to give each other some space."

After a few moments of silence Heather said, "Fine. Here's you some space." The line went dead.

Jack was relieved that the relationship was over. Running the pub and being the Can Man was only made harder by having a girlfriend. He knew he would miss her but watching over cops on their beats at night was more important to him.

The next day while getting the pub ready for the off-duty cops, Chief Mike and Officer Taylor walked in and sat at their usual spots at the bar. Jack poured them both a beer.

Chief Mike said, "Jack, I have a couple of things to tell you. Number one. I have promoted Officer Taylor here to Sergeant."

"Wow, that's great!" Jack said.

Turning to the new sergeant, Jack shook his hand and said, "Congrats Officer Taylor. You certainly deserve it after being on the force for over 20 years. Exactly how many years?"

Officer Taylor looked at Jack and said, "Let's just say it was over 20 years and leave it at that."

The three laughed and Jack poured himself a beer. They toasted the occasion.

Jack turned his attention back to the Chief. "You said you had a couple of things to tell me."

"Oh yeah, there is one more thing."

Even though the Chief suspected Jack was the Can Man, Jack didn't think it would be about that.

Chief Mike said, "Well Jack, I just hired two new police officers. And they are a team."

Jack thought, *what does that mean?*

The Chief continued. "I hired them right out of the Academy. They went through training together and I thought, heck I'll just take both of them."

"I can't wait to meet these new men," Jack said.

"Well, you got it wrong, Jack. They're not men. They're both women," the Chief said with a smile. "And don't worry. I told them about your pub and the free second beer policy."

"That's fantastic," Jack answered.

Chief Mike went on. "Wait, Jack, there's more. They were both at the top of their class in marksmanship and scored high on all of their tests. The mayor told me to hire them before some other department got them. And since I told them I would take them both, they couldn't say 'no.'"

Jack asked, "When can I meet these two?"

The Chief smiled and said, "They just came in."

Jack looked up at the front door.

The new officers were both about 5'10" tall and in great shape, like most twenty something-year-olds. But that wasn't the half of it. One was the darkest African-American he'd ever seen and the other was a redhead with ivory skin.

Jack and the Chief both waved the new recruits over to the bar. The Chief shook both their hands. "Welcome to Suzanna's Pub. This is Jack, the owner."

He shook their hands and said, "I am so happy to meet you both and welcome to my pub. Like the Chief has told you, your second beer is on the house. It's an unwritten rule here that law enforcement gets that special." They both smiled and looked around at the pub. Jack, of course, kept it clean and all the flat screen TVs were tuned to a sports channel.

"We like it already," they both said at the same time. Everyone laughed. Jack then turned to Chief Mike and asked, "Well, are you going to tell me their names?"

"Yes, I will," the Chief answered and pointed to the tall African-American first. "This is Officer Sasha Bademosi and this is Officer Firella Almond."

Jack looked up at the Chief and said, "Come on, what are their real names?"

Mike laughed and said, "Those are their real names."

Jack looked at them as they smiled and nodded yes.

"Okay, I want to hear your stories about these names."

Sasha went first. "Both of my parents are from Nairobi and Sasha seemed like a pretty name. They said I was a pretty baby."

"I thought I detected a little accent," Jack said.

"You are correct. I was born here but my parents had thick accents. As I grew up, I picked up some of their accents."

Jack turned his attention to Firella. "Now, come on, is that really your name?"

She laughed and said, "Yes, that's really my name. My parents both had red hair. They were the only redheads in their high school. Everyone sort of pushed them together. They ended up getting married and I was their first baby. And of course, I had really red hair. At the hospital when the nurse raised me up, the light behind my head made it look like my hair was on fire. That's how they came up with Firella."

Everyone laughed. Jack told them he loved their stories and they were always welcomed at the pub. Jack had already forgotten about his break up with Heather.

It was a fun night at Suzanna's Pub but the truth was he needed to be thinking about how to get to Lobo before the police nabbed him. He had learned a lot between Jose and Lupe. Also, Monday was coming up and that would give him another chance to talk to Jose. Jack knew Lobo made everyone nervous, but he had to do what he had to do. Jack's nocturnal activities did not produce any sightings of Lobo.

Chapter 5

Every night Jack checked on the cops walking their nightly beats and then went to the bayou area to look for the gang. Even with his night vision binoculars, he still didn't catch sight of them. Jack knew they were nomadic and probably in another part of town. That was fine with him. He would bide his time. He knew they would be back again. Jack figured Lobo was letting things cool down from where they murdered that meter reader.

Monday morning before the pub opened, Jack caught himself looking out the window for

Jose's delivery truck. That's when he heard a knock on the glass front door. He looked up and saw a nicely dressed, elderly African-American woman. His first thought was *someone needs directions*. He unlocked the door and said, "Good morning, how can I help you?"

She asked, "Are you Jack Warren?"

"Yes I am."

Jack was a little taken back and continued, "Do I know you?"

She asked, "May I come in?"

"Yes, yes, of course. Have a seat. Would you like a bottle of water?"

"No thank you. I'm fine. My grandson was murdered near your pub. I heard that the girl who survived the attack ran in here and you helped her."

"Oh yes, she did. There were two off-duty police officers here and they immediately ran down there to help your grandson. The paramedics came to help her."

"My name is Eunice. I just came from my grandson's funeral. He was a good boy. His name was Marcos Jackson. I called him Marky. He was always my favorite grandchild. He wanted to be a policeman and help people. But he had some medical issues and wasn't able to join the force. He was told he could be a meter reader, which is a division of the police department."

Jack started to feel sorry for the lady. "I never got to meet Marcos, but I'm sure I would've liked him, Eunice. Your grandson saved the young girl's life and is a hero to the city."

She looked down at her handkerchief and said, "I wanted to stop in and meet you and thank you in person for all you did to try to save my grandson."

Jack shook her hand and gave her a little hug. "I'm sorry for your loss."

After Eunice left, Jack locked the door behind her and went back behind the bar. He tried to look at some paperwork but he couldn't think about work. He pushed it aside and looked up into nothingness and thought, *that poor lady. Lost her favorite grandson. Marcos just wanted to be a police officer and help people. He wanted to be a police officer!* That was the last thing the Can Man needed to hear. If there were any doubt left in his mind about Marcos not being a police officer, that was gone now. As far as he was concerned, Marcus was a policeman and the Can Man would take care of Lobo.

Again, there was a knock at the front door. It was Jose. Jack thought so hard about what had happened he didn't even hear the delivery truck pull up. He ran around the bar and unlocked the door.

"Sorry, buddy, I didn't hear you pull up."

"Mr. Jack. Maybe you should get your ears checked. My truck has squeaky brakes."

They both laughed. Jose took the first full dolly of beer to the back cooler. Jack thought about questions he had for Jose and how to ask them without making Jose nervous. Jack decided to wait till Jose took his last load to the cooler. Jose rested his dolly by the bar. "It looks like it's going to be another hot one."

"You got that right," Jack answered. "Let's hope it makes people thirsty."

They both laughed. Jack handed Jose a cold bottle of water.

"Thank you very much," he said as he took a long swallow. His shirt was soaked in sweat. He looked up at Jack and said, "I heard the police haven't found Lobo and his gang yet."

Jack was happy Jose brought up the gang instead of him. "Yeah, but they are still looking. They will screw up or someone will spot them and they'll get caught. I just met the meter reader's grandmother. She came in just before you arrived. The poor lady is devastated."

Jose said, "My church is praying for his family.

Jack couldn't hold it any longer. He asked, "Have you heard anything else on Lobo?"

Nervousness immediately came over Jose's face.

"As I told you before, Lobo is a bad man and everyone at my church is afraid of him. I've heard nothing new. We just hope he gets caught or goes back where he came from." Jack knew that Jose was afraid and decided to drop the subject.

"Jose, don't work too hard in this heat. I'll see you next time."

Tilting back his dolly, Jose said, "Okay, thank you."

Jack continued to think about Lobo and his gang. He wondered why no one had spotted them yet. There were only two reasons he could come up with. One, they had left town; or two, they purposely stayed out of sight. Then he remembered the attack on Lupe. She said they came from under the overpass. It was nice and dark under there. Maybe they stayed out of sight in the daytime and don't come out until dark. If that's true, that would be great because that's when the Can Man is out on patrol. Jack figured they laid low in one of those abandoned brick warehouses during the daylight hours and then ventured out at night.

The more he thought about it, the more he got a mental image about how they operated. They were like vampires. They slept during the day and attacked at night.

Chapter 6

Throughout the next week, everything was normal and quiet. Jack spent time thinking about his murdered wife, Suzanna. She was the reason he now wears a disguise and roams from rooftop to rooftop at night to watch over cops. He also thought about Heather. He was glad they broke up. Now he could do his Can Man nocturnal activities without trying to hide them from her.

The Can Man went out to check on a policeman on his beat, when he caught sight of a little light. He crouched down and inched closer to the building's edge to look down into the dark alley that ran between the two old warehouses

Jack didn't see anything. He pulled out his night vision binoculars and looked again. He was on top of one of those three story buildings and had a great vantage point. And just like that, "boom," the gang emerged from the basement stairs. One smoked a cigarette. That must've been the light Jack caught sight of. There were five members of the gang. None of them looked like Lobo. Lupe had told Jack that Lobo looked like none of the other gang members. She said he had sandy curly hair, had a fair complexion, and didn't have any tattoos.

Jack continued to watch as the five stood around the stairwell. They looked around as though they were watching for something. Jack thought *maybe this isn't Lobo's gang.* After a couple of minutes, they stopped talking among themselves and faced the stairwell. Jack zoomed in for a closer look.

Someone headed up the stairs in the alley. Jack still couldn't get a clear view because gang members were in the way. And then, just like that, Lobo appeared. This was the first time Jack had laid eyes on him. This guy was big. He had on a leather vest and no shirt with dark pants and construction boots. And like Lupe said, he had sandy curly hair.

Lobo said something to his gang and they all looked up. Jack couldn't believe it. He thought he was well hidden. Jack heard the gang as they made their way up the squeaky fire escape. Jack ran at a full sprint to the other side of the rooftop where he knew there was another tight rope. To his horror, it was gone. He looked back and saw Lobo's gang appear. Luckily, there was another way down, a second fire escape in front of Jack. He knew if he jumped onto it would be noisy but but he had no choice.

There wasn't any time to take the stairs. He slid down the handrails. The metal slats on his disguise came in handy for sliding. Jack figured they heard him. He jumped to the ground from the top of the last flight of stairs. He had no time to exit the alley. If there ever was a time to need his Can Man disguise, this was it.

Jack immediately crouched down by a row of trash cans. He pulled in the metal slats on the inside of his poncho and lowered his trash can lid hat. Now, he looked like the rest of the trash cans in the alley. It was too dangerous to peek out from under the hat.

Jack heard the gang as they came down the fire escape. If they found him, they would surely kill him. Jack thought about how Lobo killed people. He slit open their stomachs. *Man, oh man*, Jack thought. He would give everything he owned to be somewhere else right now.

The gang was now on the ground in the dirty alley. Jack barely breathed. Lobo shouted something in Spanish and the others started kicking over trash cans. They made a lot of racket. As they got closer to the Can Man, Jack held his breath. His trash can lid hat was securely fastened to his head and he braced himself and tensed up for the pull he expected. He felt a hand on his hat. He squinted his eyes and waited. Lobo shouted once again in Spanish. At his words, the hand let go.

The sound of retreating footsteps as they left the alley may have been the best thing the Can Man ever heard. Jack knew Lobo was smart. He remained still. That was the plan for now. After about 20 minutes, he thought it was safe to exit that alley. When the gang kicked over the trash cans, it released a lot of stinky garbage. Being in a dead-end alley didn't help. The air inside his disguise was hot, stale, and smelly.

Jack was about to get up when he heard a voice from above. It was Lobo. Apparently, they ran around the other side of the warehouse, ran up three flights on the fire escape and came back over to watch the alley from above.

Wow, Jack thought. *That was a close one.* Lobo was crazy, smart, and sly. No wonder many people feared him to the point they wouldn't even talk about him.

After a long time, Jack figured it was safe to move. He peeked out but he didn't see anything. Then a light rain started. That was a good thing. It would mask any noise he made as he went up the fire escape on the next building. All he wanted to do was get back home to his apartment.

Chapter 7

Jack packed the Can Man outfit back into the cedar chest, and made his way to the bathroom to take a hot shower. He stood under the water and thought about what happened. For the first time his disguise was used not to watch others but to save his life. He was close to having his belly sliced open and being left to die in that alley. Lobo was no one to be taken lightly.

Jack dried off, put on his pajama bottoms, and walked into his small kitchen. *A scotch on the rocks sounds good right about now.* He opened his mostly barren pantry. Jack held up a big bottle of scotch and saw it was almost empty. He put it back in the pantry.

The next morning, Jack had errands to run. He needed to go to the grocery store and the liquor store. As he picked up some meats and cheeses for sandwiches, he felt a tap on his shoulder. He turned around and it was Firella. Jack couldn't stop his big smile.

"Firella, what a nice surprise running into you. Are you getting all settled in at your new job at the station?"

Smiling back she answered, "Yes, I am, thank you for asking. Chief Mike has been terrific with Sasha and me. We are his favorite salt and pepper team. Actually, we are his only salt and pepper team," she laughed.

Jack then asked if she and Sasha were ever coming back to his pub.

She responded, "Of course. We have been really busy getting settled in at the station and finding a place to live.

"Jack asked, "You two are getting a place together?"

Firella answered, "No, no. We both had to find our own places to live."

"Well, it was great seeing you, but I still have to make a scotch run, go home to drop everything off, and then get to my pub. Don't be a stranger."

Firella answered, "Don't worry, I will come by. And maybe someday I can help you with that scotch."

With that, Jack made his way out of the supermarket.

Jack arrived at his pub about 15 minutes before opening time. The daytime regulars were waiting for him. When he unlocked the front door, they followed him in. After he had everything up and running, he thought about Firella. *Was she hitting on him when she said she wanted to help him with his scotch or was she only playing?* He snapped out of his daydream. He wiped down his bar and thought about Lobo.

Jack now knew why no one had seen them and even more important, he knew where they were. Lobo was a mad dog and needed to be put down. But he was surrounded by his gang. And Jack's rule is that he only kills cop killers. He couldn't kill the other gang members because of association. He needed some way to separate Lobo from his gang. That wouldn't be easy.

That night, Can Man would go out and observe the gang. *At a distance,* he laughed to himself.

The next night at the pub, things were extremely busy. Jack looked up at the bar and almost every seat was taken. He then looked at the tables. They were all full. Jolene and Betsy had their hands full. Between the TVs, jukebox and everyone's conversation, it was a noisy place. About that time, the bar's phone rang. Jack dried off his hands and answered.

"Hello, Jack. I hope I'm not disturbing you." It was Heather.

Jack thought, *I don't have time for this.*

"Hi, Heather. Actually, I am real busy now. The bar is almost full."

She said, "I'm sorry. I won't keep you. I just thought we should talk."

Jack responded, "Okay, I'll call you soon. Got to go now." He hung up. He thought, *she really is a great gal, but she would be better off with some guy who can give her all the attention she deserves.*

From behind him Jack heard a female's voice, "What does it take to get a beer around here?"

Much to Jack's happiness, he found himself looking at Firella sitting at the bar. She smiled at Jack and he could not hide his grin.

"Firella, I'm so happy to see you."

"I told you I would come visit you."

"Yes, you did. What's your pleasure?" Jack asked.

She looked at him for a moment and said, "Just pour me a lite beer."

"Coming up," Jack said, as he spun around to go to the beer taps. He grabbed an ice cold beer mug from his refrigerator and tilted it under the beer tap to not have too much foam. *Why am I so happy to see Firella? That's a stupid question. You know exactly why.* He liked Firella and he thought, *I think she likes me, too.*

Jack walked back to Firella and kept an eye on the beer. He had filled it to the brim. As he arrived, he reached for a coaster and tossed it down in front of her. He still smiled when he sat the beer down and looked up at her. She smiled back. Then everything went into slow motion. Sitting next to her was none other than Lobo.

Many thoughts raced through Jack's mind. She said something to him, but he didn't hear it. His smile was long gone.

All he could manage to get out was, "May I help you?"

Lobo answered in a heavy Spanish accent, "Give me a draft beer."

Jack left and grabbed a mug off the counter. He thought, *no cold glass for you.* When Jack walked back, Firella was at a table with some fellow officers. *This is a good thing,* Jack thought. He sat the beer in front of Lobo. Then came a question Jack didn't want to hear.

"Is this the place where that woman ran into that got mugged behind here?"

Jack didn't want to lie. Lobo might already know the answer. "Yes, it is." Jack waited for the next unwanted question.

"What did she say to you?"

Jack thought he could end this conversation.

"She said she was mugged and I called the paramedics for her. That's about it."

Lobo drank the whole mug in one gulp and looked at Jack. He had the eyes of a killer.

Jack asked, "Would you like another?" Lobo put down some money on the bar and walked out. Jack picked up the money and thought, *all these cops in here and a cop killer just walked in and had a beer right in the middle of them.*

Firella returned. She hopped up on the bar stool and asked, "Where did your friend go?"

"He is not my friend. He's just a customer."

Firella answered, "Well, anyway he asked my friends over there if you were the owner."

Jack pretended not to be interested but inside he was concerned. *Now I'm on Lobo's radar.* That was the last thing he needed.

Chapter 8

As Jack drove home that night, he decided to take the long way to his house. There wasn't any sense in letting Lobo know where he lived and how close it was to the pub. That night Jack didn't sleep well. Too many Lobo thoughts raced through his mind. The next few days were uneventful. The Can Man laid low.

Jack had the sneaky suspicion that Lobo and his gang were watching the rooftops for the Can Man. After the alley incident, this was the second time he felt he was being hunted. And Jack didn't like it. He made the decision to not cower down to that mad dog. That's what guys like that want. They like to rule through intimidation. The cops don't get intimidated and neither should he.

Around 3 o'clock in the morning, Jack awakened to an alarm in the distance. It was a cool evening and he had left a window open. There wasn't any telling what the alarm was about. Jack jumped up and put on the Can Man disguise. He tight-roped his way over towards the alarm. Jack stopped for a moment. The next tight rope lead to an old three-story brick apartment building. They were much different then warehouses.

The Can Man had to walk on the roof's edge around the perimeter, otherwise the tenants on the top floor could hear his footsteps on their ceiling. It was possible, they would then come out to see who was on the roof. It was a minor problem.

Walking along the roof's edge was easy for him. But that wasn't the problem. The bad thing was he could be seen from down below, although at night with a black sky behind him and three to five stories up, it would be difficult for someone to spot him.

Jack moved along the edge and made his way to the mid-point of the apartment building. He looked down and saw what the alarm was all about. It came from his favorite little supermarket. The liquor store next-door was also broken into. Both glass front doors were smashed open. Broken glass was all over the sidewalk. The police were already there. Officer Chris Morgan drove up in his cruiser and talked to Officer Garza. Garza heard the alarm while he walked his beat and rushed over on foot.

Jack thought *who did this?* Then he thought *who else has a gang to feed? Lobo, of course.* He was sure because this job needed multiple people. It's possible they smashed both doors at the same time, ran in and grabbed anything and everything they wanted. They probably made a clean getaway back to that warehouse basement.

It all made perfect sense. Jack smiled at his own smartness, but all of a sudden he was illuminated from down below. Morgan and Garza had their flashlights trained on him. In an instant, he jumped backwards to get out of sight. At this point, footsteps on the ceiling were the least of his worries. He ran across to the closest tight rope and made his way as quickly as he could, and as far away as possible.

The two officers looked at each other and Officer Morgan said, "That's the second time I've seen him."

Officer Garza responded, "Wow, did we just see Can Man?"

"Yes we did," Chris answered. "He is real." Chris continued, "That guy saved my life a few years ago and as far as I'm concerned, I didn't see anyone."

Officer Garza responded, "You're not going to get any argument out of me. I'm still not too sure what I think I saw, or how to describe it. Besides, last time I checked it wasn't against the law to stand on the edge of the roof." He patted Officer Morgan on the back and said, "Let's finish up here."

The Can Man was out of breath when he made it back to his apartment. Jack couldn't believe he got spotted. He also didn't know if the two cops below would report the sighting. He put away the Can Man disguise and decided to let things cool down for a few days. He also listened in on conversations at the pub to see if there were any talk of the Can Man sighting.

The next few days were uneventful. Jack felt a little relieved. One thing he did notice was that Firella always used to come in with Sasha. Now, lately she came in alone. *Jack thought, could Firella be interested in me?* He had recently got out of the relationship with Heather. Jumping into another one was the last thing he needed. On the other hand he was a little attracted to her. He thought, *Maybe I could somehow start this relationship with the understanding that I like to have my nights free.* Jack would have to give it some thought. The next day, as he was opening up, one of his early regulars, Big Don, asked Jack if he saw all the police activity down at the Bayou.

Jack asked with all seriousness, "What are you talking about."

Don replied, "I don't know what happened. But it must've been big. There were lots of police cars, yellow tape everywhere, and a coroner's van."

Oh no, oh no. Jack thought. Please Lobo, please tell me you didn't kill a cop. He picked up the phone to quickly call Jolene to come in and cover for him. She said "no problem" and was there at the pub shortly thereafter. Jack met her at the front door and said, "Thanks for coming over, Jolene, on such short notice. Something bad happened down by the Bayou again. I want to walk down there and see what's happening."

Jack walked at a fast clip and thought about how brazen Lobo was getting. For example, he broke into two stores at the same time and walked into a bar full of cops and had a beer. It's like he wanted to show his gang he was brave. Jack arrived at the taped off area and felt sick when he saw that it was the exact same place where that mad dog killed the meter reader.

From behind a wall, Jack spotted Officer Sasha and Firella. They saw Jack and walked over. Jack noticed that both of them smiled as they walked over.

That told him that it wasn't one of their own that met an early demise. Sasha spoke first.

"Jack, what are you doing here? You're supposed to be at your pub."

He said, "One of my customers told me there was some police activity right here behind my pub. And I was hoping and praying it wasn't a police officer that got hurt or worse."

Sasha replied, "Don't worry, Jack. It wasn't one of us. It actually was a low-level drug dealer that had been known to run in a local street gang.

Firella walked over to Jack and patted him on the back. "Thank you for caring about our well-being. But we are okay and are able to take care of ourselves just fine."

Jack felt a little silly. Would he jump every time he heard a siren or saw some yellow tape? Firella was right. He said, "You're right. I know the police can take care of themselves. I guess I better get back to the pub."

Firella took Jack's arm and walked him a few steps away from Sasha and said, "Don't work too hard and I'll come see you after I get off."

Jack got that feeling again that maybe Firella was flirting with him. Although he was a little smitten with Firella, his main concern was Lobo. This guy had really gotten into Jack's head. That mad dog needed to be put down fast. But the big question was, how to isolate him from his gang and do it in a place where the Can Man could do what the Can Man does... kill cop killers?

Chapter 9

Later that afternoon, Jack wiped down the bar and looked up at the clock. The last daytime regular was gone and the off-duty cops would come in soon. Firella danced through his mind and he looked out his windows for her. There was no one in the pub but him. It was the little quiet he had every day. The last thing he needed was to jump into another relationship. He couldn't get Firella out of his mind.

The little bell above the door rang and in walked Chief Mike and Sergeant Taylor. Jack looked at the clock and saw that it was almost 5 o'clock. He filled their mugs, then walked over to their favorite spot at the bar and sat down their beers. The three talked and more customers came in. Jolene and Betsy also arrived and went right to work.

By 6 o'clock, there was a good crowd, but no Firella. Jack thought she made him wait on purpose. Maybe she had some other reason for not being there. The only thing that should have been on his mind was taking care of his customers. He went back to serving his customers and was at the register when he heard the little bell ring. He turned around, ready to see Firella walking in with her beautiful red hair, but it wasn't Firella. It was Lobo. Jack's face changed.

Lobo walked over and sat at the bar.

Jack asked, "May I help you?"

Lobo said, "Give me a draft beer."

Jack already knew what he wanted but he tried to get him to talk. Talking wasn't Lobo's style. That made him a little scarier. No one knew what was on his mind. Jack heard someone loudly clear their throat at the other end of the bar. He looked that way and was surprised to see Firella. Jack was so engrossed with the Lobo encounter that he didn't even hear the bell. He tried not to walk too fast. But like a child headed for candy, Jack went over to her.

"Hi, Jack," she said with a big smile. "I told you I was coming here. Sorry I'm a little late."

Jack responded, "You are not late. You can come here anytime, any day."

She laughed and said, "Well that's good to know."

Jack brought over her favorite brew in a chilled mug and sat it down on a coaster.

Firella said, "I had some paperwork to do on the murder down at the Bayou."

He thought this was a great time to learn more. "Too bad about that guy. You said he was some kind of a drug dealer?"

"Yes, that's right." She continued, "He was also known to run with a loosely knit street gang. Their numbers are small. Now they are smaller."

Jack was ready to ask a big question and hope she would give him some info.

"Can you tell me what happened? If it is going to get you in trouble, you don't have to."

"No, no, it's okay. Everyone at the station knows you and consider you one of us. And by the way, they told me what happened to your pregnant wife. I'm so sorry."

"Thanks, Firella."

"That guy was really butchered."

"What do you mean?" Jack knew exactly what she meant but he wanted her to tell him. He wanted to know that guy's stomach had been slashed open. That was Lobo's trademark.

Firella leaned forward and spoke in a hushed tone. "I don't mind telling you, but it is a little gory."

"No, please go ahead."

"Well, he was all cut up and they even slashed his midsection open."

"Aargh," Jack responded but he tried to act surprised. He leaned back with his hands held up, and said, "That's enough."

Firella thought she had really shocked Jack and that's precisely what he wanted her to think. He had confirmation that it was a Lobo killing. Of course he wasn't going to tell her that.

"Okay, stay right here. I've got to go check on my other customers." As he walked away, Jack thought *Firella would be the one who would be shocked if she knew the murderer was sitting down at the other end of the bar.* Lobo's head was down. He looked at his beer like he was thinking about something or maybe just resting. Jack thought, *yeah I guess robbing and murdering people must be exhausting work. The truth is that stuff is a police matter. When you murdered that meter reader thinking he was a policeman... Well that's a different story. That's when the Can Man gets involved.*

Jack asked Lobo, "Do you want another draft?"

Lobo nodded yes. Then he paid when it arrived.

Jack thought, *Okay that's his second beer. He always leaves after his second beer. And never tips. He is very predictable like that.* Jack stopped in his tracks. *Lobo always comes in on*

Thursday. Maybe this is when he takes a little time off from the gang he led. And this is the only time he is alone. This could be the window of opportunity the Can Man was looking for—Lobo without his gang protecting him.

Jack worked his way back down the bar, wiped it clean and picked up empty mugs. He came to Firella.

She asked, "Did you miss me?"

Jack smiled at her and said, "Of course. But I've got to take care of my customers."

She said, "This is your business and I think you're doing a great job." She smiled back at him and said something he didn't want to hear from her. "I see that guy is back at the other end of the bar."

Jack immediately had two thoughts. One: she was watching him. As in she was interested. And two: The last thing he wanted was to bring the spotlight over on Lobo.

He answered her and said, "Oh, he is just a regular guy who drops in every once in a while. He is quiet and doesn't talk much or bother anyone." After playing down Lobo, it was time to change the subject. "Are you watching me walk up and down the bar?"

A guilty smile crept on her face. She raised her hand. They both chuckled. He asked her if she would like a refill.

"Of course," she said. "This is the free one right?"

Jack responded, "You better believe it."

He put her empty mug with the others to be washed and grabbed her a chilled one from the freezer. He stood at the tap and glanced towards Lobo's seat. He was already gone. Only an empty mug remained. Of course he didn't leave a tip. Jack thought, *That's fine. Go back to your tribe. Tonight I learned your weak spot.* The Can Man now knew when he would get Lobo. He still didn't know how.

Chapter 10

A few days later, Jack was in his favorite local supermarket. He put some oranges into one of those clear bags they leave out for customers. Jack felt a tap on the shoulder. It was Miguel, the produce guy.

"Hello, Miguel. How are you today?"

Miguel answered, "I am fine." Then he looked down and said. "Well, not really fine."

Jack looked puzzled and asked, "What's wrong, Miguel?"

After a pause, Miguel said, "Did you hear about the break-in we had a few weeks ago? It was done by a ruthless gang that stays in our area. And they are now threatening us if we talk to the police. They come in, they take food without paying and sometimes they even take money from the cash register. I am telling you this because I wondered if they did that to you?"

Jack put his hand on Miguel's shoulder and answered, "No Miguel, they are not doing that to Suzanna's Pub. It's probably too crowded with off-duty police officers to try that there. All I can tell you is that the police are looking for them and hopefully they will be caught soon."

Jack and Miguel talked a few minutes more, then Jack left. As he drove back to his apartment, he thought about how Lobo and his gang had brought pain and suffering to his neighborhood. He wanted to tell the police where their hideout was, but if he did that, he wouldn't be able to get Lobo.

The Can Man needed to meet him soon and put an end to this. So far he knew it would be a Thursday night while Lobo was away from his gang. But not when he was at Suzanna's Pub. Jack thought, *how do you kill a cop killer in a pub full of off-duty police officers?* He needed to give that one some more thought.

A few nights later, Jack wiped down his bar like he had done a million times before. He looked over his pub full of customers. He thought how lucky he was to have many friends from the police station. And of course, he was grateful for his two waitresses, Jolene and Betsy.

Jolene was engrossed in a conversation with Officer Alford. She wasn't taking an order, but chatting away with him. Come to think of it, he had seen them hanging around each other. He was glad they were friends. They both certainly had been through some tough situations. Jolene's friend, Maria, turned out to be a cop killing sniper and was later found dead on a rooftop. Officer Alford had his police cruiser shot up by her. She barely missed him. It's about time they had some happiness. Jack wished them well to himself.

Jack thought about his own situation with Firella. He lit up when she came around. Then he laughed at himself. *What a stupid pun...*

Firella lights him up. Oh well. She did. He found himself wishing she worked nights instead of days. If she worked nights, he would be able to date her and be free to do his Can Man duties while she was on her shift.

Later that Wednesday night, Jack poured a beer and looked over his crowd of customers as usual. The beer tap sputtered. That meant he had to go to the walk in cooler and bring out a fresh keg.

The old dolly he used since he bought the pub, finally broke down. He had to carry it out by hand and a full keg is heavy. He would need help. Officer Alfred was at one of the tables. He was young and fit. Jack caught his eye and motioned him over.

Alfred said, "Hi Jack, what can I do for you?"

"I was wondering if you could help me carry a fresh keg out here from the cooler?"

"Of course," he responded.

As they walked back to the cooler, Jack said, "I don't even know your first name."

"My first name is Alfie."

Jack looked at him and said, "No really, what is your first name?"

"That really is my first name. I think my parents had a good sense of humor."

Jack chuckled, "Yes, I guess they did, Officer Alfie Alford."

They walked into the large cooler. The heavy door closed on its own as usual to keep the cold air in. Jack pointed towards the back where there was a stack of beer kegs. "I need one of those."

Both men bent down and got a firm grip on the keg and lifted it together. At the door, a metal rod stuck out with a round flat piece of metal attached at the end. This was designed to allow someone coming out with their hands full, to hit it with their hip and the door would open. Jack hit the rod. The keg was heavy but the two men made it back just fine. They sat it on the floor in front of the beer taps. Jack said, "Thank you, Alfie for your help. I couldn't have done it without you. Let the house buy you a beer."

"No, no, that's okay. The house already got my second beer and I need to get home." Officer Alford stopped over by Jolene and whispered something in her ear before he walked out.

Good, Jack thought. *They made a nice couple.* He went back behind the beer tap with a fresh keg loaded in. Jack poured all the backed up beer orders. His thoughts reverted back to Lobo. *How do I get Lobo?* All he knew was Lobo was there alone on Thursday nights for two beers. Many ideas raced through his mind. He could put poison in his beer. But that would mean having a dead Lobo on his hands with him holding the beer mug. No, that was not an option. He could cause a fire or an explosion that would make everyone run outside, then he could kill Lobo. But that was a terrible idea. Suppose everyone didn't rush outside to see or worse, Lobo rushed out to see. Nope, that was another dead end idea.

About that time, Betsy walked up to the waitress station and asked for three bottles of light beer. Jack slid back the door on his reachin cooler. He noticed there was only one left. "Betsy, I've got to go get some more out of the cooler. I'll be right back."

Betsy said, "No problem."

Jack said, "Hey, that's Jolene's line."

She answered, "Yeah I know. She says it to me so much that she's got me saying it."

"That's funny. I'll be right back."

Jack walked into the cooler. It was a little dark but he could see enough to find a beer. He reached down to pick up several six packs and mumbled to himself. *It's dark enough for someone to get mugged in here.* He stopped and looked up.

Could this be the answer he had been looking for? What a perfect little secret spot. He could take out Lobo right in the middle of a room full of cops. He was so excited about this new revelation that he ran back to the bar without the beer he went for in the first place.

Betsy looked at him and said, "Well?"

Jack felt like an idiot. "I'm sorry, Betsy. I was thinking about something else. I'll be right back again only with the beer this time."

After things settled down at the pub, with running out of bottled beer and having an empty beer keg, Jack thoughts went back to Lobo. He now knew when and where, but there was still a question. How in the heck would he get Lobo into the cooler with him? The next day was Thursday, but Jack wasn't sure if he was ready.

Jolene walked up to the waitress station. She said, "Jack have you got a minute?"

"Oh, I thought you had a beer order," Jack answered.

Jolene said, "I guess you have noticed Officer Alford and me talking a lot lately. And I have a question for you."

Jack said, "Yes, I noticed a little. But that is your business and as long as you're happy, I'm happy. Now what is the question you have for me?"

"Next week is Alfie's birthday. I really like him. I was thinking of throwing him a little surprise birthday party here. What do you think?"

Jack responded, "I think it's a great idea. Do you want to have a cake with candles?"

Jolene looked shy. "I was thinking of something a little over the top. A little more exciting."

"Okay, you have my attention now. What do you mean over the top?"

Jolene answered, "I was thinking we could rent one of those giant big fake cakes that I could jump out of. You know, maybe wear a bikini and have a sash that says 'Happy Birthday Alfie' on it. What do you think?"

"I think it's a fantastic idea. And I'm pretty sure everyone would love that. Especially Officer Alford. What day were you thinking about having the party?"

"I was thinking next Wednesday. It's the middle of the week and no one would be expecting it."

Jack thought quickly. "Could we make it Thursday? It would be better for me."

"'No problem." She walked away.

Jack thought, *this is perfect.* A party could be the diversion he was looking for. While all of the off-duty police looked at Jolene as she popped out of the cake, he could take care of Lobo in the walk-in cooler. But how could he get Lobo in there? That would take some more thought.

Chapter 11

The next night was Thursday. He looked up at the clock and it was almost 8 p.m., the time Lobo came in for his two beers and his away time from his gang. But Lobo was a no-show. Jack thought, *this is terrible. Did he and his gang leave town? Did you get caught?* Jack's mind raced. He finally told himself to calm down and give it a rest. There were as many answers as there were questions. Whether Lobo was a show or no-show, that party would still go on the Thursday of next week. He still didn't know how to get Lobo back there, but that was still in his plan.

The weekend came and went. Monday morning arrived and Jack paid bills like always. About then, Jose drove up in his beer delivery truck. Jack jumped up and unlocked the door for him. Jose gave his usual happy greeting.

Jack said, "Good morning" and went back to paying his bills.

Coming back through from his last load of beer, Jose stood up his empty dolly and said, "I don't see your dolly back there. Where is it?"

Jack replied, "Oh, it finally broke. I haven't had a chance to get a new one."

Jose said, "You know I still have my old one. Would you like to have it?"

Jack said, "That would be great. That would save me some money."

Jose said, "When would you like me to bring it over?"

Jack said, "How about Thursday?"

Jose asked, "Don't you want it sooner?"

Jack said, "Thursday works best for me." And left it at that.

Jose waved and said, "See you Thursday."

Then Jack jumped up and locked the door behind him. Unbeknown to Jose, he may have filled in the missing piece of the puzzle. This could be how to get Lobo into the cooler. After all, he did it with Officer Alford. Why couldn't he do it with Lobo?

About that time the bar phone rang. Jack answered it, "Suzanna's Pub. How may I help you?"

It was Jolene. "Jack, I rented a cake for me to jump out of."

Jack asked, "Where in the heck did you find one?"

She answered, "At the great big party store they opened up in one of those empty warehouses down the street."

Jack said, "Oh yeah, I saw that." He remembered seeing the store on one of his nightly excursions. *The Can Man sees a lot of stuff.* He went back to his conversation with Jolene. "When do you want to have that thing delivered and what time are you thinking of jumping out?" Jack knew Lobo shows up around 8 o'clock p.m. Even though he was a no-show last Thursday, he still had to plan as if he would show up.

Jolene asked, "What time do you think?"

Jack said, "How about a little after 8 o'clock p.m., maybe 8:10?"

Jolene laughed and sarcastically asked, "Are you sure you don't want 8:11?"

Jack said, "Okay, okay. You asked. I thought a little after 8 p.m. was a good time."

Jolene agreed and said she was just teasing him. Then she added, "They will bring the cake over on Thursday around 2 o'clock p.m. And they will also set it up. We can drape a sheet over it to hide it from prying eyes."

"Sounds good," Jack said and then hung up the phone. The plan was coming together. He walked back-and-forth behind the bar as he saw everything fall into place.

Thursday afternoon rolled around. Jose stopped by with the used dolly. Jack thanked him. All of his daytime regulars were there. Jack opened the bar cooler door and rocked the keg below the beer taps. It was a little less than half full. *Good.* Jack wanted it to run out of beer. This was going to be tough. All he could do was give it his best shot. As the last of his daytime regulars left, Jack picked up their empty beer bottles and mugs. He wiped down everything. About then a guy walked in wearing a dark gray jumpsuit.

"We're here to deliver a party cake and set it up for you," he said.

Jack said, "Yes, I've been expecting you."

Then the guy asked, "Where do you want it set up?"

Jack looked around and thought, *I want all of their backs towards the beer cooler.* He pointed to the opposite side of the room and said, "Over there. Right next to the wall. I'll move those tables and chairs for you."

The guy held up his hand, "No, don't worry. We got this. There are three of us and we do this kind of stuff every day."

That was okay with Jack. They moved a couple of tables and chairs. They had the cake moved in and set up in about 15 minutes.

"That's it. We'll be back tomorrow to pick it up at about the same time," the man said.

"Great," Jack answered. "See you then." Jack looked over at this great big pink birthday cake and thought, *Two great things would happen tonight. Jolene will surprise Officer Alford, and the Can Man would surprise Lobo.*

Jack draped the cake with the sheet that Jolene brought over earlier. He thought about Jolene. She really was a good person. But, Jack had bigger things on his mind. The timing had to be perfect. There were many moving parts. Jack still felt good about his plan. He looked up at the clock. It was a little past 5 p.m.

Chapter 12

J olene arrived at the pub. She wore a robe. "I've got my bikini on under here. I need to get inside the cake before everyone arrives."

Jack pulled the sheet off the cake and Jolene climbed in. Jack gave her a bottle of water before recovering the cake. Minutes later, Chief Mike and Sergeant Taylor walked in and sat down at their usual spot. Jack brought them their beer mugs.

"Hey guys, welcome. How was your day?"

The Chief spoke first, "Same stuff, different day." Sergeant Taylor nodded in agreement.

Jack said, "Well, I've got something to tell you that may brighten up your day." He now had their attention. "Tonight at 8 p.m., Suzanna's Pub is throwing a surprise birthday party for Officer Alford."

Then Sergeant Taylor said, "His birthday was Monday."

"Yes, that's right. But that's why it will be a surprise."

Both men seemed politely interested. Jack added, "We have a giant birthday cake."

Still no real interest. The Chief watched the TV.

Jack thought, *Time to pull out the big guns.* "And Jolene will jump out of the cake wearing a bikini."

Now he had their undivided attention. The two men looked at each other.

The sergeant spoke first. "What a great idea, Jack. I will do my best to drop back by here for that."

Jack and the sergeant looked over at the Chief.

The Chief said, "Yes, of course. I'll do my best, too. I'll be back for the surprise birthday party."

Jack said, "Great!"

He walked back down the bar and thought, *Everybody is lukewarm on the party until you tell them Jolene will be in a bikini. But that's okay.* It was important to have a lot of people watching Jolene. That is the time he would lure Lobo to the back cooler.

The pub began to fill up as usual. Jack had spoken to Officer Martinez earlier that day to see if he could make sure Officer Alford would be there for his surprise birthday party.

Martinez said over the phone, "Don't worry, Jack. All he talks about is how he can't wait to see Jolene."

"Thanks. I've got to go now.." Jack said. He and then thought to himself, *Alfie will really see Jolene tonight.*

Jack watched the clock a lot now. He kept running over everything in his mind. He didn't need the Can Man outfit for this plan. But he did need his special knife. He had placed it above the door inside the walk-in cooler. It was almost 8 p.m. and Jack was a little tense but confident. He had done everything he could to make this happen. He thought, *Jolene has been inside that cake for almost three hours. That's a long time.* He hoped her legs could still jump after that long wait.

Still no Lobo yet. Jack had already decided that if Lobo was a no-show again, he would have to figure out another time. As Jack took a draft beer order, the tap started to spit. He knew the keg was low, but Lobo wasn't there yet. He reached into the bar cooler and pulled out a bottle of the same draft beer the customer wanted. He put it on a coaster and said, "It's on the house." He would need to change the keg soon.

Jack stalled some more. *C'mon Lobo*, he thought, *I can't have an empty keg with a room full of customers.* The little bell above the door rang. With all the noise, nobody heard it but Jack. It was Lobo. Jack was relieved, but not home, yet. Lobo sat down on a bar stool. It was a little after eight. Five more minutes before Jolene jumped out. It was time for Jack to uncover the cake.

Officer Alford sat at a table that was full of his fellow officers. He looked at them and asked, "Why do I feel like there is something going on here? And what's with that giant pink cake over there?

Officer Martinez answered, "I don't know. Let's walk over to it and take a look."

Jack looked at the clock again. It was 8:08 pm. Time to start the plan. Jack walked up to the beer tap to pour Lobo a beer. It started spitting like he knew it would. He let it spit and cough because he wanted Lobo to hear it.

He walked back to Lobo and said, "I'm sorry, sir, but my keg has run out. It will take a moment to change it."

Lobo didn't seem to care. Jack walked towards the big cooler then he spun around and pretended he had forgotten something. He walked back over to Lobo and said, "Excuse me, but I was wondering if you could help me bring out another keg. My dolly is broken."

Lobo gave Jack an ugly look and said in a heavy accent, "I don't come here to work."

Jolene would pop out any second now. Jack thought quickly and made him an offer. "It will just take a second and all of your beers tonight will be on the house."

Lobo acted like he was really put out but agreed to help. About the time they entered the cooler, Jolene jumped out and there was a roar from everyone as they clapped and shouted.

Lobo said, "What's going on out there?"

Jack ignored his question and pointed to the keg on the floor. As Lobo took a step forward Jack reached up behind himself and got the knife. Lobo's back was to Jack as he bent over the keg. He spotted the dolly. He said, "Hey, there's a dolly right there."

By then it was too late. Jack was now in full Can Man mode. His blade was already under Lobo's neck.

Lobo froze with his back still to Jack. He asked, "You are the man we chased off the roof?" Jack leaned towards Lobo's ear and said, "And you are the man who killed the meter reader."

Lobo's eyes widened and that was the last thing he heard.

Jack pulled Lobo's body over onto the dolly and took it to a spot he had cleared out in the back of the freezer and put a tarp over it. He would deal with it later. He grabbed the keg and rolled it out of the cooler.

Two customers saw him struggling with the keg. They carried it the rest of the way out to the bar and waiting party.

Jack thought to himself. *There's good news and bad news. The good news is Lobo is no more. The bad news is Jolene has already put her robe back on. I'll take that trade any day.*

After hooking up the full keg, Jack went about the business of taking care of his bar customers. Both the Chief and the sergeant came over to Jack and shook his hand, "Thanks," they both said.

Jack nodded and said, "Of course. My pleasure. Thanks for coming back."

Sergeant Taylor then added, "Thanks for telling us about the surprise. I had no idea Jolene was so...so, well she is very attractive."

Once again, Jack said, "Thanks for coming back."

Jolene sat in her robe at Alfie's table. Jack was at the bar thinking. Around three in the morning, he would take Lobo on the dolly and roll him down to the Bayou, one block behind the pub and dump him in. The bayou could take him down to the Gulf where the sharks are waiting.

Jack walked over to the table where Alfie and Jolene sat. Alfie jumped up and shook Jack's hand and said, "Jack, thank you so much for hosting this surprise party for me. All of you really caught me by surprise."

Jack said, "That's why they call it a surprise party."

Jolene stood up, hugged Jack, and said, "Jack if anyone can pull off a good surprise party, you Can...Man. Then she slung open her robe and gave Jack a surprise.

Thanks to my sister, Denise Ditto Satterfield, Author of *The Tooth Collector Fairies Series* *www.toothcollectorfairies.com. I could not have done it without you.*